The Adventures of
Eddie and Flip Boy

Published by Brolga Publishing Pty Ltd
ABN 46 063 962 443

PO Box 452
Torquay Victoria 3228
Australia

email: markzocchi@brolgapublishing.com.au

National Library of Australia
Cataloguing-in-Publication data
        Bobby Holland Hanton, author.
        ISBN 9781921596247 (paperback)

A catalogue record for this
book is available from the
National Library of Australia

Printed in Australia
Cover design by Luke Harris, Working Type Studio
Typesetting by Scott Riddle

BE PUBLISHED

Publish through a successful publisher
National Distribution to Australia & New Zealand
International Distribution to the United Kingdom
Ebooks Worldwide
Sales Representation to South East Asia
Email: markzocchi@brolgapublishing.com.au

The Adventures of Eddie and Flip Boy

Written by Bobby Holland Hanton

Illustrated by Katerina Kojeva

Chapter 1

Eddie was supposed to be getting ready for school. Instead, he was watching his favourite program on TV — Flip Boy! Flip Boy was about to attempt a running double forward **somersault**, with a twist. It was a big moment.

"Eddie!" shouted Eddie's mum. "Eddie! Have you forgotten about school?"

"What?" says Eddie. His wide eyes hadn't left the screen.

"School! You're going to be late!" Mum's face was red. "And don't say 'What?', say 'Pardon me beautiful Mummy, I didn't hear what you said'." Eddie's finger hovered over the pause button. He wanted to see just one more backflip.

"Shoes on Eddie — and make sure you turn the TV and bedroom light off!" said Mum as she grabbed her coat.

Instead of turning the TV off, Eddie pressed the pause button, leapt over his bed, flicked the light off and **screamed** out into the hall at top speed.

Mum was waiting for him at the front door.

Eddie's mind wasn't really on the job in maths. He couldn't wait to get outside at morning recess and try a few of Flip Boy's moves.

Before long the school bell rang for morning break. Eddie was first out the door, his mind racing with ideas on what to try first — a backflip or a walking handstand? He tried a standing backflip...but face-planted onto the hard ground. **Ouch**!

"How embarrassing," Eddie thought to himself.

"Maybe I'm going to need a bit of practice."

Eddie limped back into the classroom and for the rest of the day he stared at the clock. He found it hard to listen to his teacher and couldn't wait to get home to watch the rest of Flip Boy.

At last the bell rang and it was time to go home.

Chapter 2

Eddie raced through the back door, dropped his bag, screamed straight past Mum and through the door into his room. He found that the TV had been turned off.

"Muuuum!" yelled Eddie with pain in his voice. "Why did you turn the TV off? I was watching Flip Boy this morning and now I've missed it all!"

He stormed back down the stairs in a **huff**.

Mum had her hands on her hips. "Eddie, it's rude not to say 'Hello lovely Mummy' when you get home. And I asked you to turn off your light and your TV this morning, and that didn't happen, did it? Eddie, we have rules in this house and I'm not seeing any respect or discipline from you at the moment."

Eddie was confused by a couple of big words.

"Um…what is respeck and dissypen?"

Mum slowed down her speech. "Res-pect and disc-i-pline, Eddie. They mean that you have to **listen** to others and work hard," said Mum seriously.

"Whatevs Mum. Can I watch Flip Boy now?"

Dad sighed one of those parent sighs that means 'we've had enough of this.' "You can watch Flip Boy once you have had dinner, done your homework, brushed your teeth, your room is tidy and you've got your pyjamas on," he said.

"Oooookay," moaned Eddie. He would do just about anything to watch Flip Boy before bed.

Next morning, nothing much had changed. Eddie was slowly getting ready for school when he noticed someone drop a flyer in the letter box.

Eddie could hardly contain his excitement. He ran up to Mum, jigging from side to side and jumping up and down all at once.

"Mum, mum, mum — take a look at this! It says Flip Boy is doing a 'Meet and Greet' in the city next Saturday. Can I go, can I go can I go can I can can can…." stammered Eddie, unable to finish his sentence.

"Well, we'll see. If you promise to be good — I'm sure your father will be happy to take you," she said, looking across at Eddie's dad with a wink.

"Oh, ah, yes, well, let's see little man. If you can do a bit more listening to us and a little less lazing around at home, I'll take you to see Flip Boy on Saturday."

"**Yesssss**. Thanks Dad, thanks Mum!" Eddie smiled from ear to ear.

On Friday night, Eddie put himself to bed at 7.30pm on the dot. His parents couldn't believe it — he had brushed his teeth, put his dirty clothes in the laundry and tidied his room. They looked at each other in amazement.

In the morning, Eddie was **raring** to go.

"Wake up Dad! Come on, it's Flip Boy Day! Let's have breakfast and get going!" yelled Eddie into his dad's ear.

"Huh. What, who, when?" Dad was still mostly asleep. "Go back to bed son!"

"No Dad, we've got to get going! I want to be first in line to see Flip Boy!"

By 7:00am, Eddie and his dad were on the train to the city.

Chapter 3

It was super busy at the exhibition where Flip Boy was appearing. There were people everywhere. Eddie and Dad were **shocked** to find a very long line had already formed, snaking around the whole stage area. They had no option but to line up and wait their turn.

Eddie wondered whether he would ever get to the top of the queue.

"Maybe I should have got up even earlier, Dad. This is going to take ages!"

"We can always go home," offered Dad.

"No way Dad! We are staying here till we meet Flip Boy…and that's that!" exclaimed Eddie, striking a typical Flip Boy pose.

After two hours of waiting without getting anywhere, Eddie's feet started to hurt and Dad's old footy knee was playing up. But still they waited.

Four hours.

They could see Flip Boy now. One more hour and they were getting close!

Then, the **unthinkable** happened: a security guard appeared and made an announcement.

"Thanks for coming folks, Flip Boy is sorry he can't meet everyone today but he'll be back another day and perhaps you can meet him then."

Eddie looked in astonishment at his dad. He felt tears in his eyes and his bottom lip strated to quiver. Eddie thought his dad's head might explode!

Dad said, "This is **CRAZY**! We have been in this line for five hours, and just as we get to the top, you tell us Flip Boy is going? You can't do this to me...I mean my son...you just can't."

"I'm sorry sir, but there's nothing I can do," said the security guard.

Eddie began to sob, and his dad was upset too.

"Come on son, let's get out of here."

They stumbled out through a side door into a lane and Eddie accidently bumped into someone walking briskly towards a waiting car. Eddie, already feeling sorry for himself, hit the ground with a thud.

"Hey Muscles, sorry about that. Are you OK?" said a familiar voice from above.

Eddie looked up. It was Flip Boy! He was standing right there!

"Oh, er, wow...Flip Boy is it really you?" Eddie quickly wiped away his tears.

"It is **me** buddy! You look a little upset," said Flip Boy.

"I'm okay, I thought I wasn't going to meet you. Dad and I waited for so long, and then they said you had to go," said Eddie, standing up now, eyes wide.

"I'm so sorry little man. I didn't think so many people would turn up! I have another Meet and Greet to go to now — thank you so much for coming today. Would you like a quick selfie with me and then maybe you can tell me a little about yourself. How does that sound?"

Eddie was over the **moon**!

"Yes please Flip Boy, that would be great!"

Flip Boy and Eddie talked for a full five minutes, all about how Eddie watched his TV show every day, his school, his family, what he ate for breakfast — everything! Eddie told Flip Boy that he tried to do some of Flip Boy's tricks, but often hurt himself when they didn't work.

"Let me tell you a secret Eddie," whispered Flip Boy. Eddie was all ears.

"I wasn't good at my tricks either, at the start. I started doing gymnastics and martial arts lessons when I was young. I kept going to my classes, building my confidence with discipline and hard work. If you love it, and keep working, you can do

anything! Look at me now, I'm a **Superhero**!"
Eddie drank in Flip Boy's words.

"So Eddie, ask your parents to take you to a gym class, or karate or taekwondo, or all three! Have fun and you'll be better than me in no time! And one more thing before I go — make sure you concentrate at school — and help Mum and Dad at home," he said, winking at Eddie's dad. And with that, Flip Boy was gone.

"Dad, did you see that?! I just met the actual Flip Boy and he said I need to find a gym class! When can I go Dad? When, when, when?"

"It's been a long day son. Let's go home and work it all out with Mum."

Chapter 4

Eddie and his dad arrived home, weary but **pumped**.

"Hello beautiful Mummy!" said Eddie as he burst through the door. "Have we got a story for you!"

They told Mum everything that had happened — all about the long wait, the security guard and then accidentally bumping into Flip Boy. Mum was amazed, and delighted to see Eddie so happy and talkative. And polite.

The next day, Dad picked Eddie up from school in his car.

"I have a surprise for you Eddie. I'm taking you to your first gymnastics class!"

If Eddie's smile could wrap around his whole head, it would have.

"Oh wow, thank you, thank you, thank you wonderful Daddy!"

Eddie was a bit nervous when they arrived at the gymnasium. There were kids as young as four there, right through to grown adults. Eddie wasn't sure where to look or even where to go. Would he be good enough to do some of the **incredible** tricks and moves? Dad sensed Eddie's doubts.

"Now Eddie, it's normal to feel a bit nervous on your first time here. I know you can do this — go and enjoy yourself and make Flip Boy proud," said Dad in his calming voice.

A coach saw Eddie and came over.

"Hey, you must be Eddie. Nice to meet you."

"Yes, I'm Eddie. Nice to meet you too. I'm a bit nervous," said Eddie.

"Nothing to worry about at all Eddie. Let's go and meet the others and get you going."

Eddie looked over at his dad, who gave him a reassuring nod and a wink. Dad watched proudly as Eddie threw himself into some basic gymnastic moves. Eddie was listening hard and picked it up quickly.

After the lesson, Eddie ran over and said, "Dad, did you see me? That was so much **fun!** Can we come again tomorrow. Please, please, please?"

"Yes, of course we can come tomorrow. I saw how much you were enjoying it."

Chapter 5

Over the next few weeks, Eddie worked hard at his gym classes and continued to improve his moves and his confidence. His mum and dad loved his attitude and that he never wanted to miss a class. Flip Boy's words about hard work and discipline made Eddie determined to do his best.

Eddie's school teacher also noticed his improvement — so much so that she asked him to play a special role in the school play. Not just any role — Eddie had to **rescue** a kitten that was stuck up a tree!

"No problem!" thought Eddie – Flip Boy did the exact same thing in one of his TV shows. Maybe Eddie could rescue the cat the same way that Flip Boy did it?

For the three weeks before the school play, Eddie practised and practised and practised. His parents were impressed by his dedication and were so proud and happy that he was so passionate about something. The big day loomed large.

"It's the school play tomorrow Eddie. How are you feeling?" asked Eddie's mum.

"I'm **super** excited Mum!" exclaimed Eddie. "I reckon I'm ready to go — I've worked so hard."

"Are you even a little bit nervous?"

"Well. Yeah. I am actually," admitted Eddie. "I've never done this before. I hope I can do it on the day."

"You've worked so hard Eddie. I'm sure you'll be fine," said Mum.

The next day, Eddie woke up early and got ready for school. He felt butterflies in his tummy, and wondered if he really could do it.

Finally, the school day finished and everyone gathered in the school hall for the play. Parents began to arrive. Kids were getting into costumes and chattering backstage. The **excitement** began to build.

The show started well, and all the parents were laughing and crying at the right moments. Eddie's big scene was coming up. He waited nervously to make his entrance.

In his mind, he pictured the moves that he had practised so many times. But...someone had moved the tree! It was in a different place to where they had rehearsed. What would Eddie do?

"What would Flip Boy do? An extra **backflip**! That will get me to the tree!" thought Eddie.

He heard his cue.

"Oh no, please someone help me! My kitten is stuck up the tree and might fall! Help!"

Eddie **burst** on to the stage.

"Never fear! Eddie Boy is here! Stand back everyone while I save the kitten!"

With the bright spotlight following him, Eddie flipped, twisted and somersaulted across the stage. He added the extra backflip and leapt high into the air, almost in slow motion, and **plucked** the kitten out of the tree — nailing the landing in a typical Flip Boy pose.

"There you are Ma'am. Your kitty is safe and sound. If you ever need a real live Superhero, just call for ol' Eddie Boy!"

The audience **gasped** and were completely silent for a moment, unsure of what they had just seen. Then, almost as one, they rose to their feet, clapped, whistled and cheered for Eddie Boy, a real life Superhero for a moment in time. The noise was so loud, Eddie thought that the roof might blow off!

Eddie looked to the back of the school hall, through all the stamping and clapping and cheering and saw a figure standing near the exit door.

To Eddie's amazement, it was Flip Boy, clapping and cheering with the rest of the audience. He gave Eddie a thumbs up and a grin that said 'Well done young man — look where hard work gets you'.

And, with that, Flip Boy was gone.

The End

Flip Boy's Five Fabulous Exercises

If you can do all the exercises on the next few pages, you are a **LEGEND**!!!

And if you're feeling strong, you can do them all again.

See if you can do each exercise five times in a row and then move on to do the next exercise five times in a row and the next...wow! You are a **Flip Boy Hero**.

Maybe you can even get Mum or Dad or a friend to do them with you?

Push-ups

These will make your whole body strong, especially your arms so you can lift heavy things. Push ups can be done with a straight body or on your knees.

Sit- ups

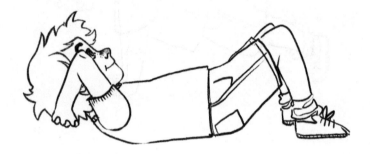

Sit-ups make your back and tummy muscles stronger. When these mucles are strong you will be better balanced and your spine will be protected from injury when playing sport.

Sit-ups

Squats

Squats are for strong legs, so you can run and jump. Bend from the knees and try to keep your back straight.

Squats

Star Jumps

These will keep your heart strong and your body fit.

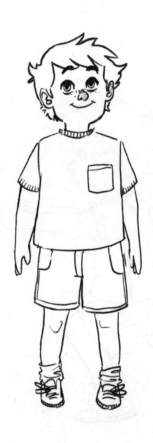

Star Jumps

The Plank

This will keep the centre of your body strong so that everything works well together. Hold the plank and count to five.

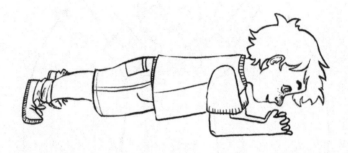

Food and other Great Stuff

Did you know that most of your body is made up of water? Cool huh? You need to give your body water every day to keep it working well. Make sure you sip on a bottle or glasses of water throughout the day to give your **body** what it needs. It's what makes plants grow and people need water to grow too.

Give yourself a fun **challenge** and see how many different coloured fruit and vegetables you can eat every day. They will keep your body strong and healthy.

At the end of a great day, when you have done your exercises and watered and fed your body well, the last thing left to do is **sleep**. Sleep helps our brain and body rest and grow. Good night!

About the Author

Bobby Holland Hanton

Bobby Holland Hanton is a Hollywood stuntman. He has worked on blockbuster films, including *Thor, The Avengers, Mission Impossible, Star Wars, Skyfall, Batman, Captain America* and *Pirates of the Caribbean*; as well as hit TV show, *Game of Thrones*, winning multiple awards and appearing as the stunt double for actors such as Daniel Craig, Chris Evans and Chris Hemsworth. Bobby trained as a gymnast from the age of four, and he's passionate about the mental and physical benefits of enjoying exercise from a young age. Inspired by his experiences with his daughter, this is his debut picture book.

About the Illustrator

Katerina Kojeva

Katerina is a Bulgarian illustrator, jeweller, and costumer who works in feature films in the UK and USA. Now London based, she works in the Costume Department full time but has loved drawing and painting all her life. Following her passion, she is making the transition to full time illustrator. This as her first children's picture book.

The Adventures of Eddie and Flip Boy
Bobby Holland Hanton

			Qty
ISBN: 9781921596247			
	RRP	AU$15.99	.....
Postage within Australia		AU$5.00	.....
		TOTAL★ $_____	
		★ All prices include GST	

Name: ....

Address: ....

....

Phone: ....

Email: ....

Payment: [ ] Money Order   [ ] Cheque   [ ] MasterCard   [ ] Visa

Cardholder's Name:..

Credit Card Number: ....

Signature:..

Expiry Date: ....

Allow 7 days for delivery.

Payment to: Marzocco Consultancy (ABN 14 067 257 390)
                   PO Box 452
                   Torquay Victoria 3228
                   Australia

BE PUBLISHED

Publish through a successful publisher.
Brolga Publishing is represented through:
• National book trade distribution, including sales,
marketing & distribution through Simon & Schuster.
• International book trade distribution to:
    - The United Kingdom
    - Sales representation in South East Asia
• Worldwide e-Book distribution

For details and enquiries, contact:
Brolga Publishing Pty Ltd
ABN 46 063 962 443
PO Box 452
Torquay Victoria 3228
Australia

markzocchi@brolgapublishing.com.au
(Email for a catalogue request)